This Orchard book belongs to

____

____

____

For Kevin, who loves Christmas!
with love, Giles

For Father Christmas,
with love, Emma

ORCHARD BOOKS

338 Euston Road, London NW1 3BH

Orchard Books Australia

Level 17/207 Kent Street, Sydney, NSW 2000

First published in 2013 by Orchard Books

First published in paperback in 2014

ISBN 978 1 40832 934 4

A CIP catalogue record for this book is available from the British Library.

1 3 5 7 9 10 8 6 4 2

Printed in China

Orchard Books is a division of Hachette Children's Books, an Hachette UK Company.

www.hachette.co.uk

I love you Father Christmas

Giles Andreae & Emma Dodd

I love you, Father Christmas,

In your big red suit,

With your bright silver buckle

And your black shiny boots.

Your beard

looks amazing,

And, yes, you're

rather fat . . .

. . . But you probably just like eating,

And there's nothing wrong with that!

I love your pretty reindeer,

Flying fast across the skies . . .

. . . I'll leave them all some carrots

And some yummy mince pies.

I love you, Father Christmas,

And I promise I've been good.

And I'm not just saying that

Because I know that I should.

I've tried every day

To be as helpful as can be.

I've said my 'please' and 'thank you's

And I always eat my tea.

I've played very nicely

With all the girls and boys.

I've kept my bedroom tidy

And I've tried to share my toys.

And I know I'm very lucky

With the way my life has been

But, it's just . . . I do like presents,

If you're getting what I mean?

So, lovely Father Christmas,

If you visit us tonight,

I swear there'll be no peeping

And we'll switch off every light.

Yes, I love you, Father Christmas,

You're the best, you are! Yippee!

Oh, I hope you like this letter . . .

With lots of love

from ME! xxx